Cosmo
THE DODO BIRD™

Cosmo is a dodo. He is one of a unique species of bird that once lived on our planet. Hundreds of years ago, he and the other dodos lived peacefully on the island of Mauritius, isolated from man and their charted land.

Approximately 300 years ago, and only a few years after the first sailors arrived on the island, the dodos had almost completely disappeared. Only Cosmo remained. He was the last dodo.

With his new friend, 3R-V the spaceship, Cosmo now travels from planet to planet in search of other dodos like him. Together Cosmo and 3R-V have great adventures.

Originally published as *Les Aventures de Cosmo le dodo: La
recherche du joyau* by Origo Publications,
POB 4 Chambly, Quebec J3L 4B1, 2008

Copyright © 2008 by Racine et Associés
Concept created by Pat Rac
Editing and Illustrations: Pat Rac
Writing Team: Neijib Bentaieb, Isabelle Houde,
François Perras, Pat Rac

English translation © 2011 by Tundra Books
This English edition published in Canada by Tundra Books, 2011
75 Sherbourne Street, Toronto, Ontario M5A 2P9

Published in the United States by
Tundra Books of Northern New York
P.O. Box 1030, Plattsburgh, New York 12901

Library of Congress Control Number: 2010928798

Library and Archives Canada Cataloguing in Publication

Pat Rac, 1963-
[Recherche du joyau. English]
In search of the jewel / Patrice Racine.

(The adventures of Cosmo the dodo bird)
Translation of: La recherche du joyau.
ISBN 978-1-77049-245-5

I. Title. II. Title: Recherche du joyau. English.
III. Series: Pat Rac, 1963- . Adventures of Cosmo the dodo bird.

PS8631.A8294R4213 2011   jC843'.6   C2010-903168-7

We acknowledge the financial support of the Government of
Canada through the Book Publishing Industry Development
Program (BPIDP) and that of the Government of Ontario
through the Ontario Media Development Corporation's
Ontario Book Initiative. We further acknowledge the
support of the Canada Council for the Arts and the
Ontario Arts Council for our publishing program.

ONTARIO ARTS COUNCIL
CONSEIL DES ARTS DE L'ONTARIO

*For more information on the international rights,
please visit www.cosmothedodobird.com*

Printed in Mexico

1 2 3 4 5 6   16 15 14 13 12 11

MIX
Paper from
responsible sources
FSC® C101537
FSC
www.fsc.org

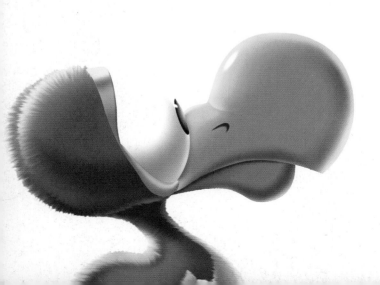

For all the children of the world

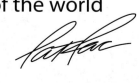

THE ADVENTURES OF
COSMO
THE DODO BIRD™

IN SEARCH OF THE JEWEL

Tundra Books

Cosmo is awakened by his spaceship, 3R-V.

"Life up ahead! Life up ahead!" 3R-V is very excited.
It has been ages since either of them saw anything but stars.

"What a beautiful planet," Cosmo says, wiping the sleep from his eyes
and taking the controls. "Prepare for landing!"

"Will do, Cosmo – the dodo-gear is down. It should be a smooth landing!"

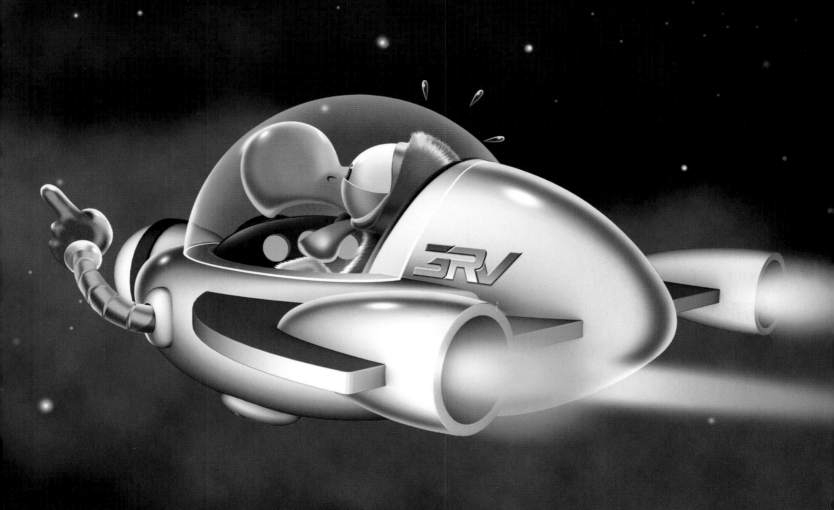

But the landing is not smooth at all.
The surface of the planet is dotted with holes.

Finally, 3R-V manages to land safely. Cosmo is so excited that he doesn't waste a minute before hopping out of the spaceship. "This is a wonderful place!" he shouts. "There must be other dodos living here."

"I don't know how many dodos there are, but there certainly are a lot of holes!" says 3R-V. "I wonder why!"

Suddenly, the planet begins to quake. A long crack appears under Cosmo's feet, and an enormous corkscrew twists out of the earth. Cosmo tries to be brave, but 3R-V is terrified. What is happening?

Out of the hole pops a strange creature. Cosmo doesn't even have time to introduce himself before the odd fellow challenges them:

"This is *my* territory. If you've come for the jewel, you'd better understand it belongs to *me*!"

"What jewel?" the space travelers ask.

"You mean you don't know the legend of the jewel?"

Cosmo and 3R-V shake their heads.

The creature pulls a scroll from under his helmet. "It's all written down right here. My great-great-great-grandfather, Diggs the First, discovered an enormous treasure," he says, "the biggest jewel ever found."

The two friends listen while the man goes on.

"Diggs the First hid his treasure on this planet. That jewel is my inheritance. The trouble is, I haven't the slightest idea where it is."

"So, that's why you're digging holes all over the place," says Cosmo.

"But who are you?" asks 3R-V.

"Why, I'm Diggs the Sixth. No one except my family lives on this planet.
Exactly who are *you*?"

Cosmo is disappointed to learn there are no other dodos living here,
but he answers politely. "I am Cosmo, and this is 3R-V."

"Well, hello and good-bye,"
says Diggs. "I have to keep
looking for the jewel. I have
a feeling it's very close!"
He begins digging again.

"I have a feeling we're closer to disaster than we are to the jewel," whispers Cosmo.
"If we don't do something to stop Diggs, his planet is going to break into thousands
of pieces."

"Let's try not to be here when that happens," says 3R-V.

Diggs disappears before their eyes.

"I don't think he has any idea of the damage he's doing to his planet. We really have to talk to him," says Cosmo.

"Shouldn't we just get out of here?" 3R-V asks, trembling a little.

"Certainly not! We have to help Diggs understand what will happen if he doesn't stop digging up the place."

"How are we going to talk to him? He's gone underground,
and we don't know where he might turn up next."

"I have an idea, 3R-V. Let's go back up into space. From there,
we'll have a better view and a better chance of finding Diggs."

The two friends circle the planet for a long time,
waiting for Diggs to poke his nose above ground.

"Well, I'll be a daffy dodo!" exclaims Cosmo.
"From here, we can really see what's happening to the planet."

"Yes we can, Cosmo, but if you ask me, Diggs is the daffy one."

"We've got to bring him up here so he can see the damage
he's caused," says Cosmo.

Cosmo spots Diggs. "There he is, 3R-V! Hurry, before he starts digging again!"

"Diggs, wait! We have to talk to you!" cries Cosmo.

"You're still here?" Diggs asks impatiently.

"Of course we are, Diggs. Come aboard.
3R-V needs to show you something."

"Sorry, my friends, but I'm busy.
I'm closing in on the jewel."

"It's very important," Cosmo explains. "The future of your planet is at stake!"

"Why does that matter? All it does is hide my jewel from me. The jewel is what counts. Soon, I'll be rich, rich, RICH!"

"What good is all that money if you don't have a planet to live on?" asks Cosmo.

Diggs isn't listening. He waves his arms, repeating over and over "My jewel, my jewel! I'll be rich!"

Cosmo has a great idea.

"Diggs, we know where the jewel is, don't we, 3R-V?"

"Er, I uh . . . no. I don't know where the jewel is."

"Yes you *do*, 3R-V." The dodo signals, and 3R-V understands that this is how to get Diggs up into space.

Diggs becomes more excited. "Are you positive you know where the jewel is? Please, please tell me."

"You'll find your treasure faster if you climb aboard 3R-V," says Cosmo.

"All right! Take me to the jewel!" Diggs buckles up, and 3R-V heads into outer space as fast as he can go.

Cosmo is left behind to hope Diggs will change the way he treats his planet.

Diggs is impatient. "Why is this taking so long? I can't waste time on a trip to outer space!" he cries.

"You have to see for yourself what's happened to your planet since you started searching for the jewel," says 3R-V.

Diggs sees how much damage he's caused. "You and Cosmo are right! I *am* destroying the planet. But my jewel! I must have it! What should I do?"

At that very moment, Diggs notices something. "3R-V, take me farther into space!" Confused, 3R-V does as he's told.

From far out in space, the planet seems very tiny. Diggs unrolls his parchment.

"This is incredible!" he cries. "From here, the planet is exactly how Great-Great-Great-Grandfather Diggs described the jewel! He said it was round and of the purest green, dotted with blue patches. I found the jewel! My planet *is* the jewel!"

3R-V grins and returns to the planet as fast as he can go.

"Cosmo! Cosmo! I've found my jewel!" cries Diggs.

"You were right! Once I was up in space, I could see how much damage I've caused. I also discovered the jewel that is my inheritance. Look! It's exactly like my great-great-great-grandfather's drawing. See? This planet is the jewel!"

Diggs catches his breath. "I must get to work! I have to fill up these dreadful holes. My planet is the real treasure, and now I know I must protect it!"

Diggs is very grateful to his new friends. "You are real heroes. You showed me where true wealth could be found. Thank you!"

Cosmo is delighted with the way everything worked out.

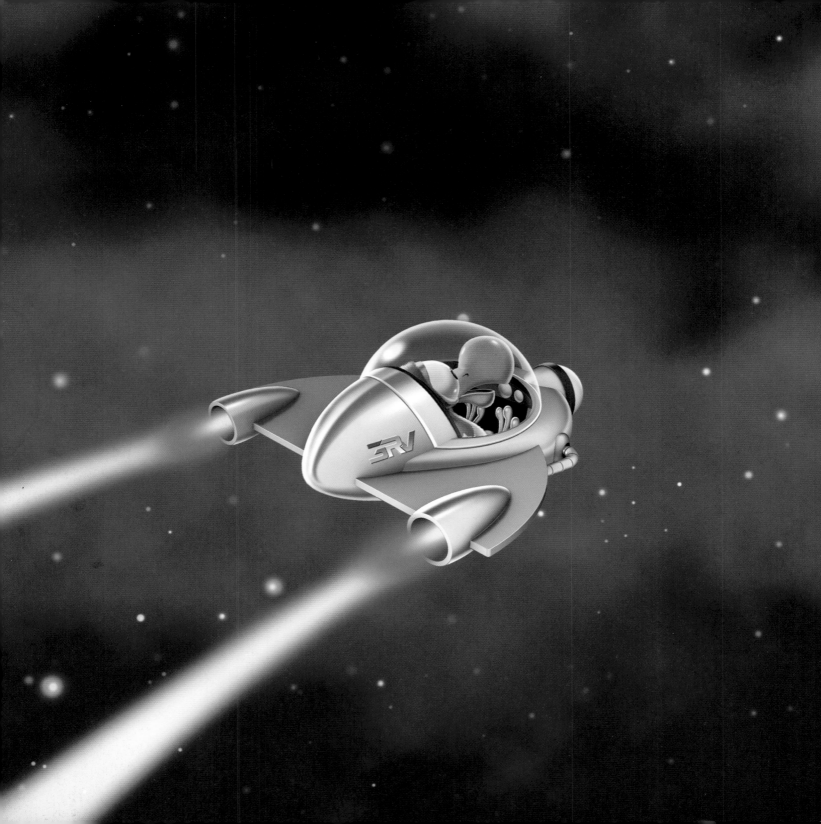

Knowing that Diggs will take care of his environment, Cosmo and 3R-V leave the planet. They haven't found any dodos, but the two friends are still searching.

"I hope it won't take so long to find another planet this time," says Cosmo.

"Me too," says 3R-V. "I don't like having a pilot who's asleep at the controls!"

3R-V is a kind and gentle robot-ship invented by a scientist
on the planet Earth. This scientist cared a great deal about nature
and the environment. He built the robot-ship according to the following
principles: reduce, re-use, and recycle. He named the ship 3R-V and gave
it a propulsion system that uses a renewable, non-polluting source of energy.
3R-V is also equipped with incredible technological resources.

3R-V is Cosmo's best friend, and, together, they travel from planet to planet
in search of other dodos.